The Old Banjo

The Old Banjo

By Dennis Haseley
Drawings by
Stephen Gammell

Aladdin Books

Macmillan Publishing Company
New York

Collier Macmillan Publishers
London

Aladdin Books
Macmillan Publishing Company
866 Third Avenue, New York, NY 10022
Collier Macmillan Canada, Inc.
First Aladdin Books edition 1990
Printed in the United States of America
A hardcover edition of *The Old Banjo* is available from
Macmillan Publishing Company.

10 9 8 7 6 5 4 3 2 1

Haseley, Dennis.
The old banjo/Dennis Haseley; illustrated by Stephen Gammell. —
1st Aladdin Books ed.   p.   cm.
"Aladdin Books."
Summary: A hardworking farmer and his son succumb to the
enchantment of some very special musical instruments that
have been abandoned on their farm.
ISBN 0-689-71380-0
[1. Musical instruments — Fiction. 2. Farm life — Fiction.]
I. Gammell, Stephen, ill. II. Title.
PZ7.H268801 1990
[E] — dc20   89-36796   CIP   AC

For Connie and for Sara

All over this farm
there are instruments
that no one plays anymore.

"I wonder if some band used to live here,"
says the farmer's boy. "I wish
we could have heard them."
"Well, they're gone now," says his father,
"and we've got too much work to do."

So up in the attic
waits an old banjo
with worn silver strings.

And a trombone lies
under a bed
with a wool sock
stuffed in its bell.

And an old piano
sits in the gray barn
with the ivory chipped on its keys—
it looks like it has
a few teeth missing.

And a violin
waits in a shed
with a bright trumpet going cloudy
and a clarinet
like a shadow left behind.

But one day
just toward evening
while the farmer and his boy are working
and the sky is the color
of a stone
the old banjo remembers
how a smiling old woman
and all her sons and daughters
used to sit on the porch
and fill the night with music.

And while it remembers
the old banjo
gives a quiet little pluck.

And across that gray farmyard
the violin
hears the banjo's pluck
and begins to stretch its bow
along its strings
like a rusty door opening.

And the banjo
hears the violin
and plucks again....

And from inside the barn
the piano hears the banjo
and it pushes down one chipped key
like the shy beginning of a giggle
and the farmer looks up from his plow
and squints and says,
"Must be the cat."

But the banjo
hears the piano
and plucks another string....

And downstairs
the trombone hears the banjo
and it starts to blow
through the sock
low and soft
like a boat traveling home
through the fog.

And the banjo plucks again.

And on a shelf
in the milking house
the trumpet hears the banjo, hears the trombone,
hears the violin, and gathers up its dreams
and makes a sound
like geese flying in
on a winter's night
and the farmer's boy looks up and smiles and
sees a cloud
floating like a wing.

And now, across the farm,
all the instruments that no one plays anymore
start to slowly lift their voices
and the farmer looks at his son,
he looks at the sky
and he says, "Well, it must be the wind...."

But the banjo rings out another string
and the moon starts to rise like a drum
the stars begin to shine like bells
so they put down their tools
and search for the sound.

They look in closets
and in sheds
and in the barn and behind shelves
while the forgotten sounds are rising
and the banjo strings are playing.

And now out in the yard
the dogs begin to howl
the cows begin to moo in the fields,
until, at last, the instruments are found.

And as it's lifted, the trombone sounds
as sweet and pure
as if it were calling from a mountain,
and the violin
cries and sings
as if the fields were filled
with dancers,
and notes fly from the piano's keys
like wild birds rising,
and one by one, the farmer and
his son take each instrument
the clarinet
and the violin
and the trumpet
and they carry them into the night!

And now all the forgotten instruments
are singing together
their sound grows clear
like glass
like bells

rolling off the moon
ringing through the stars
and weaving through that boy's,
weaving through that father's
heart.

And the old banjo
with worn silver strings
lies in the attic and listens
and the sound is so beautiful…

listen.